THE HARE AND BABOON AND OTHER STORIES

Fables from Africa

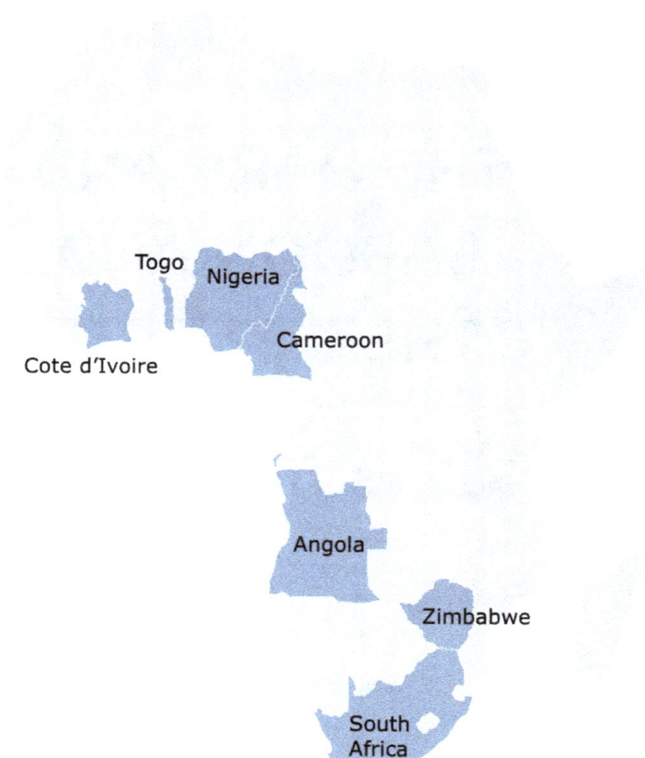

Togo
Nigeria
Cameroon
Cote d'Ivoire
Angola
Zimbabwe
South
Africa

THE HARE AND BABOON AND OTHER STORIES

Fables from Africa

By

Kandie Oriade
Hamissou Samari
Sipho Ndlela, PhD
Thamba Tabvuma
Yuri Santos
Nina Taka
Ousmane Diallo, PhD

Edited by Dr. Quinta

SQUINTI PUBLISHING

For information about permission to reproduce selections from this book, write to info@SquintiBooks.com.

Published in the United States of America by Squinti Publishing, Washington DC.
SquintiBooks.com

Illustrations by Thamba Tabvuma

Hardback ISBN: 978-1-947350-05-2
Paperback ISBN: 978-1-947350-06-9
eBook ISBN: 978-1-947350-07-6

Until the lion tells the story, the hunter will always be the hero.

Paraphrased from Chinua Achebe

Foreword by the Editor

This book is an anthology of fables from 7 countries in Africa. The countries are: Nigeria, Togo, South Africa, Zimbabwe, Angola, Cameroon, and Cote d'Ivoire.

The authors are from the named African countries, and either contributed stories they heard growing up, or translated stories told by others.

The tradition of stories being told to a hushed crowd at the end of the day remains strong in many parts of Africa. The stories serve to entertain, pass down history and culture, and also teach moral lessons to young children.

We hope these stories will provide you with a glimpse of the culture from these African countries.

Enjoy the warmth that only Africa can bring.

Dr. Quinta

Contents

The Tortoise and the Babalawo (Herbalist) – Nigeria

By Kandie Oriade

A fable from the Yoruba tribe

Avery long time ago when animals were treated equally as humans and could talk and interact with them, there lived a tortoise called Ijapa. Ijapa and his wife, Yanni Bo, lived in a small village called Ife just outside the outskirts of the Osun state. They had been married for a long time and were ready to start a family of their own but were having a difficult time conceiving. Ijapa and Yanni Bo had been to various doctors and specialists who advised them that all was well and to keep trying. They tried all avenues and options to get pregnant, but to no avail. Soon they began to get desperate.

One fateful day, Ijapa went to the market to buy some food items and on his way back home he saw an old woman with a heavy load. She was trying to place her market bag full of food stuff on her head so she could carry it home but it was so heavy that the bag fell. All the items scattered all over the market floor. With the hustle and bustle of the market goers, no one was willing to stop and help, leaving the old woman to her plight. Ijapa, who was also at the market seeing this turn of events ran up to her and offered to carry her load home. Thankfully, her home wasn't too far from the market.

Ijapa offered to carry her load home

Upon reaching her house, which was a hut made of clay, the old woman was so grateful and asked if Ijapa wanted anything in return for his kindness. Unbeknownst to Ijapa, she was a wise old woman, and she could sense that Ijapa was wanting for something desperately. It is customary in Yoruba culture not to ask for something in return of a good deed. When you are offered something, you must always refuse at first, and should only accept after multiple attempts of the offer, like a dance. This goes both ways for the offeror and the acceptor.

Obviously, Ijapa insisted that all was well, and he wanted nothing in return. After they danced over the issue of the return of favor, Ijapa finally admitted that he and his wife Yanni Bo were having issues with having children and have tried multiple venues to no avail.

The old woman then told Ijapa she knew a very powerful herbalist named Babalawo who lived across seven mountains and seven rivers in a faraway village called Oriade. She told Ijapa that if he could make the trip, which was a two-day journey to the village, then Babalawo would be able to help him and his wife. Ijapa was grateful. He thanked the old woman and ran home to tell Yanni Bo the good news. Yanni Bo was thrilled to hear the good news and urged her husband to make the trip to Babalawo the next day. Ijapa didn't mind making this trip and set out to meet this powerful Babalawo.

It took Ijapa two days as he had to cross seven mountains and seven rivers to get to the Village of Oriade to meet the Herbalist named Babalawo. Once he reached Oriade, he met Babalawo and told him of his situation. Once Babalawo heard his dilemma, he told him had a solution and would make a potent potion exclusively for Yanni Bo, and once she ate it, she would be pregnant.

When he was done making the it, Babalawo gave the potion in a calabash wrapped in a cloth for Ijapa to take it home to his wife. Babalawo advised Ijapa that this potion was only for Yanni Bo and shouldn't be touched or tasted by anybody else. Ijapa thanked Babalawo and started on his journey back home.

On his way back home with the potion, Ijapa started smelling a very delicious and tempting aroma from the cloth that contained the potion he just received from Babalawo. Ijapa was hungry and tired. He had just crossed the third mountain and third river. He had not eaten anything all day, and there was nothing around for him to eat. He remembered what Babalawo told him and told himself he wasn't going to eat it and just look. Ijapa decided to peek at the cloth to see what was inside the calabash.

Upon opening the calabash, he saw it was Efo Riro which is a bowl of thick vegetable soup rich with various fishes and assorted meats, one of Ijapa's favorite meals to eat. Ijapa was enticed. He started salivating but he thought of his wife and the warnings of Babalawo, so he closed the calabash wrapped it up in the cloth and kept on his journey.

It was getting dark as he reached the sixth river and sixth mountain. He decided to stop for a drink at the river to quell his growling stomach. Once again, the delicious aroma of the Efo Riro was tantalizing his senses. Ijapa thought to himself, *Let me check the quality of the Epo Pupa (palm oil) used to make this soup. I want to make sure Yanni Bo would eat this because she is a picky eater.*

The Epo Pupa was light orange and clear. It was a good quality. *Hmmm this oil tastes good,* he thought to himself. *Let me taste the type of fish.* He tasted a little bit more. This time he couldn't stop himself anymore. Ijapa who had been starving all day devoured this meal in a matter of minutes.

Soon after he finished the potion, he fell into a deep slumber. When he finally woke up, although it felt like he only took a nap, three days had already passed. He tried to stand up, but he felt so heavy. This was when he noticed that his stomach had grown so big, it was the size of a woman who was nine months pregnant. This obviously scared him, so he decided to go back to Babalawo's house to ask him to make him another one and to help with his growing stomach. Ijapa thought to himself, *I will just tell the Babalawo that the potion he gave me fell because I stumbled into a ditch. He is a nice man. He would make me another one.*

He wobbled his way as fast as he could back to the Babalawo's house. With both hands on his head, he began to cry and started to sing a lie as he went back to the Babalawo's house:

"Babalawo mo wa bebe (Herbalist I am here to plead)"

Chorus - "Alugbirin!" (No direct meaning)

"Ogun to se funmi ni gbaan (The potion you just prepared for me)"

Chorus - "Alugbirin!"

"To ni n mawa fowo baanu (That you asked for me not to taste with my hands)"

Chorus - "Alugbirin!"

"To ni n mawa fese baanu (That you asked for me not to taste with my feet)"

Chorus - "Alugbirin!"

"Ko to na yo mi gere (The ditch on the way)*"*

Chorus - "Alugbirin!"

"Mo wa boju wokun (My eyes met my belly)*"*

Chorus - "Alugbirin!"

"O ri tandi (My belly was huge)*"*

Chorus - "Alugbirin!"

"Mo su bu lule mo mowo baanu (It made me fall and I've tasted with my hands)*"*

Chorus - "Alugbirin!"

"Mo su bu lule mo mese baanu (It made me fall and I've tasted with my feet)*"*

Chorus - "Alugbirin!"

"Babalawo mo wa bebe (Herbalist I am here to plead)*"*

Chorus - "Alugbirin!"

"Babalawo mo wa bebe (Herbalist I am here to plead)*"*

Chorus - "Alugbirin!"

Babalawo was skeptical at first, asking Ijapa how he knew the potion was Efo Riro and why his stomach was now the size of a pregnant woman's. Ijapa kept singing, pleading on his knees and shedding tears, begging Babalawo to believe him that he really tripped on a ditch. Babalawo finally took pity on him and told him not to worry. He would make him another potion for Yanni Bo. Babalawo also gave him medicine for his growing stomach and cautioned Ijapa to be more careful this time around and sent him on his way.

Ijapa began his second journey home and couldn't wait to see Yanni Bo with his calabash of a fresh fertility potion. He had been in the Oriade village for more days than he planned. As he crossed the fourth mountain and fourth river, he started getting hungry again. It had been almost two days since he last ate. Also, he was feeling lighter and his stomach was now back to the way it was thanks to the medicine that Babalawo gave him. When he got to the fifth river and fifth mountain, he decided to stop at the river to wash his face and rest a bit. The scent of the potion wafted to his nostrils and his stomach rumbled. Ijapa thought to himself, *Let me see if it is the same type of potion that Babalawo gave me so I know it is authentic and it will work.*

He opened the calabash wrapped in cloth and saw it was again Efo Riro, but this time it was only with assorted meats. *Let me taste this meat to make sure it is not too tough for my dear wife, because I know how her teeth can be sensitive.* He dipped his hand into the Calabash and took a bite out of a juicy tender piece of meat. He soon devoured the whole bowl of Efo Riro in a matter of minutes. He washed his hands at the river and broke the Calabash to corroborate his lies that he once again tripped on a ditch, spilling the potion. Not long after, he fell into a deep sleep and when he woke up, it was three days later. His stomach was huge, and he decided to go back to Babalawo. Ijapa ran as fast as he could back to the village and when he reached

Babalawo's house, he placed both hands on this head. He wailed and began to sing:

"Babalawo mo wa bebe (Herbalist I am here to plead)"

Chorus - "Alugbirin!"

"Ogun to se funmi ni gbaan (The potion you just prepared for me)"

Chorus - "Alugbirin!"

"To ni n mawa fowo baanu (That you asked for me not to taste with my hands)"

Chorus - "Alugbirin!"

"To ni n mawa fese baanu (That you asked for me not to taste with my feet)"

Chorus - "Alugbirin!"

"Ko to na yo mi gere (The ditch on the way)"

Chorus - "Alugbirin!"

"Mo wa boju wokun (My eyes met my belly)"

Chorus - "Alugbirin!"

"O ri tandi (My belly was huge)*"*

Chorus - "Alugbirin!"

"Mo su bu lule mo mowo baanu (It made me fall and I've tasted with my hands)*"*

Chorus - "Alugbirin!"

"Mo su bu lule mo mese baanu (It made me fall and I've tasted with my feet)*"*

Chorus - "Alugbirin!"

"Babalawo mo wa bebe (Herbalist I am here to plead)*"*

Chorus - "Alugbirin!"

"Babalawo mo wa bebe (Herbalist I am here to plead)*"*

Chorus - "Alugbirin!"

Babalawo was surprised to see Ijapa again. Once again, he took pity on him and gave him medicine and made him another potion. He admonished Ijapa and told him this was the last potion he could make. He pleaded with Ijapa to be very careful not to trip and to make sure this potion was eaten by only Yanni

Bo. To make sure Ijapa did not eat the potion again, Babalawo gave him something to eat and drink, and then sent him on his way. Ijapa profusely thanked Babalawo, carried the new calabash wrapped in cloth and started again on his journey home.

When Ijapa crossed the seventh river and the seventh mountain, the smell of the Efo Riro made him salivate. He thought to himself, *Let me check what is in this Calabash to make sure that the potion is correct*. He sat down on the road path, opened the cloth, and saw the Efo Riro with an abundance of all kinds of fish and meats. Once again, Ijapa couldn't resist the aroma of this potion and succumbed to his immediate desires and feasted on the contents of the calabash. This time he took his time eating.

As he was feasting, he said to himself, *What is the worst that can happen? Babalawo is a very kind man and he would give me another medicine and make Yanni Bo another potion. I must just lie and say I tripped by a ditch.* After he was done with his meal, he once more fell into a deep slumber and woke up three days later. He felt heavy and his stomach had grown to the size of a nine month's pregnant woman. He ran as fast as he could back to Babalawo's village and once he reached Babalawo's house, he began to cry. This time he was on his knees with his hand on his head singing:

"Babalawo mo wa bebe (Herbalist I am here to plead)"

Chorus - "Alugbirin!"

"Ogun to se funmi ni gbaan (The potion you just prepared for me)"

Chorus - "Alugbirin!"

"To ni n mawa fowo baanu (That you asked for me not to taste with my hands)"

Chorus - "Alugbirin!"

"To ni n mawa fese baanu (That you asked for me not to taste with my feet)"

Chorus - "Alugbirin!"

"Ko to na yo mi gere (The ditch on the way)*"*

Chorus - "Alugbirin!"

"Mo wa boju wokun (My eyes met my belly)*"*

Chorus - "Alugbirin!"

"O ri tandi (My belly was huge)*"*

Chorus - "Alugbirin!"

"Mo su bu lule mo mowo baanu (It made me fall and I've tasted with my hands)*"*

Chorus - "Alugbirin!"

"Mo su bu lule mo mese baanu (It made me fall and I've tasted with my feet)*"*

Chorus - "Alugbirin!"

"Babalawo mo wa bebe (Herbalist I am here to plead)*"*

Chorus - "Alugbirin!"

"Babalawo mo wa bebe (Herbalist I am here to plead)*"*

Chorus - "Alugbirin!"

This time around, the Babalawo wasn't moved and didn't believe Ijapa's lies. Ijapa begged the Babalawo to save him one more time. The Babalawo turned him away with his pregnant stomach and told Ijapa he warned him to be careful and there was nothing more he could do for him. With tears in his eyes, Ijapa kept singing and pleading with Babalawo, but it all fell on deaf ears. Babalawo sent him out of his house and instructed Ijapa never to come back.

Ijapa begged the Babalawo to at least do something about his pregnant stomach. Babalawo warned Ijapa that if he gave him medicine for his pregnant stomach it would cost him. He would need something valuable to Ijapa in exchange for this medicine. Ijapa said he didn't care. He told Babalawo he was willing to pay any price for the burden to be lifted so he wasn't pregnant forever.

Babalawo said, "Because you broke my calabash, I will break your back."

Ijapa agreed to this and thought it was fair. Babalawo went back into his house and made a concoction for Ijapa to drink. After he drank the concoction, his stomach became normal, but he could no longer walk, and could only crawl and his back now looked like a cracked calabash.

Ijapa cried to the Babalawo, "You lied to me! This is not fair. You said you would only break my back and now I cannot walk anymore."

Babalawo laughed at Ijapa and told him he was a fool to believe he would be honest with a liar like Ijapa. Babalawo told Ijapa that the price of a broken back would mean he could no longer walk. Because Ijapa sang lies to him, Babalawo took his voice so he can never lie to anyone again. Babalawo kept laughing and left Ijapa to his fate as he slammed the door in his face. This is the reason why the tortoise has a cracked shell and is one of the slowest animals.

Next time you see a tortoise, ask it, "Why do you have a broken back?" It may tell you this story.

As with every fable, the moral of this story is to be content and not be greedy. If Ijapa (tortoise) had listened to the instructions of the Babalawo (herbalist), he and Yanni Bo would be happy and have gotten what they desperately wanted.

A story told by my Mom from memory.

Patience Means Waiting For Food To Cool Down – Togo

by Hamissou Samari

A fable from the Tem Tribe

O nce upon a time, very far away and deep in the African savanna stood Lakaza, a peaceful and prosperous kingdom. Every single thing within its borders had a soul, a mind, and a voice of its own. It was believed that animals and humans could speak to and understand each other. Trees could cheer, dance to melodious breezes, and smile to the rising and setting sun. Mountains and hills in Lakaza would happily move to make way for sweet and cool wind for residents during hot seasons, or to block waters in order to reduce flooding on rainy days. Rivers could switch their flows and run to helping prevent natural disasters or minimize soil erosion.

Even stones and woods *a priori* inept and insensitive had emotions and could team up to fight common enemies or fend off predators. Swords, bows, and arrows would willingly and singlehandedly go hunting or go to wars to protect their human masters. Abstract concepts could speak on their own, defending their rights and fighting for what they felt mattered to them.

Lakaza residents were wealthy, so wealthy that it was considered an affront to the gods to dress lightly—without gold-engraved footwear, gold-ornated hats, or gold clothing. It was considered sacrilege to visit sacred temples or make sacrifices to divinities in non-golden platters. If they dare to disobey, they should be prepared to live with an incurable curse for a lifetime. Generations of Lakazans had endured inexplicable ills as a sign of divine maledictions for breaking the rules.

Women in Lakaza were considered the finest creatures there were as they were all believed to have been shaped in the image of the goddess of beauty. He who dared question that would be forever condemned with only having male children and deprived of the joy of ever birthing female offspring. Or worse, he could have daughters, but should be prepared to lose them at early ages.

Men, on the other hand, were believed to be the boldest and strongest creatures ever made. They were so strong that at age 14, each teenage boy had to undergo a daunting ceremony of initiation to adulthood, which included, among other challenges, fighting a ferocious wild animal of the elders' choosing, lifting a boulder three times their weight, or pulling barehanded a sacred talisman strategically hidden deeply inside a beehive by oracles. He who dared dodge the ceremony would forever be damned with no woman to marry.

In short, *lakaza*, which literally means "do good" or "be a benefactor" in the Tem language, also rhymed with peacefulness, plentifulness and graciousness. However, the wealthiest among the wealthy, the most gracious among all, the strongest among the strong, the most admired of all men in Lakaza was their venerated ruler, Ouro-Izzaru or King Izzaru. *Izzaru*, which means the month of March in the Tem language, was the king's birth month and also his name. His golden throne stood at the base of a thousand-year-old sacred baobab tree at the heart of the kingdom. Hundreds of able men, along with ferocious animals, stood day and night underneath the old tree to assure the throne's security and cater to the royal family's needs.

Ouro-Izzaru rose to the throne at a young age after the passing of the former king, his elder brother. It was believed that Ouro-Izzaru was so gifted that he was ahead of his age and would dominate all kids his age at every challenge.

He was deliberately matched up with a dreadful buffalo

Legend had it that he underwent the ever-dreaded ceremony of initiation to adulthood at a tender age of 12. He was deliberately matched up with a dreadful buffalo of the tropics, which he defeated in record time, and only suffered a deep tear on his testicular bursa, which caused a significant loss of blood. He refused assistance and insisted that the wound remain open to attest to his bravura and undefeatability for his contemporaries and generations to come.

"The flesh and soul of Lakaza shall never surrender to a serf, be it human or a wild animal. Let it forever be known that the noble son of Lakaza has battled the king of savanna and prevailed," said the twelve-year old boy, comfortably sitting on the neck of the motionless animal and proudly holding with a firm grip both horns as a sign of domination. The animal looked dead cold. "May this scenery outlive its witnesses and be passed through future generations, and may it forever symbolize our grip over the kingdom of the wild and that of the domesticated." He concluded before being carried triumphally on the shoulders of bewildered spectators.

For the moment the young man was on top of the animal food chain, he wasn't in a hurry to come back to reality. Surrounded by his overjoyed friends and relatives, he suddenly improvised and intonated a few self-glamorizing and self-motivating lyrics, which the rest of the audience picked up in unison almost as though it was previously rehearsed:

"I am unmatched in the world of humans and that of the wild
Bring it on, you beast, and I will crush you with my bare foot
Bring it on, you king of the jungle, I'll step on you with my boots
I am unmatched in the world of the good and that of the devil
Bring it on elephant, and I will put your life in peril
Bring it on panther, and I will kill you

> *Bring it on lion and I will proudly step on you*
> *I am unmatched and will be remembered forever"*

Eventually, while the tear on his testicle had healed, it left two significantly indelible scars on himself and on future generations.

First, to mark that momentous event, upon rising to power, the young king decided to showcase his powers by ensuring that each and every baby boy born to his lineage would one way or another immortalize his battle and victory against the buffalo with a very unique stamp. Indeed, from that time on, every baby boy of his blood lineage would show a minor superficial and painless scar on his testicular bursa at birth, which would automatically fade away on the seventh day. This has remained to date the material piece of evidence as to who is the true descendant of King Izzaru and thus qualified to eventually run for the throne succession.

Secondly, and probably as a result of that testicle injury, the young king had lost his ability to procreate. Upon rising to power, the then seventeen-year-old king was urged to get married as a necessary step to sowing his royal oats and perpetuating his greatness. He married the beautiful and wealthy Dongoli. Dongoli is short for *kudongoli* because she was born on a *kudongoli* which means Monday in the Tem language. It took weeks of consultations and search for the royal family to finally select Dongoli out of tens of equally beautiful and qualified young women.

As per customs, a night long dance party was organized underneath the sacred baobab tree, and led to the king's selection of Dongoli to be the queen. Dongoli's grace, kinship and special family connections with the royal family had prevailed over other considerations and gave her a significant edge over other competing bachelorettes.

The young royal couple would spend three years together without a child. Worried and impatient, uncles and aunts advised the young monarch to marry a second wife as they were convinced that Dongoli was the infertile one. The cocky and narcissistic king hesitantly obliged, but only on the condition that he be the one to make his selection. Within days, searches were launched for the king's second wife. Days later, another big dance party was held at the royal court.

This time, Kalama was the chosen one. Kalama is short for *kalamaazi* because she was born on a *kalamaazi,* which means Tuesday in the Tem language. Kalama's family was known as one of the largest and most fertile of Lakaza. The royal family and advisers were convinced in her ability to have inherited those precious genes and to help the king achieve that lifelong dream of his.

Izzaru, Dongoli, and Kalama lived together for another three years with zero children. This time, Izzaru's sisters raised their voices and insisted that they pick a wife for their brother. The king accepted the idea, but on the condition that no one else, but he himself, pick the woman for him. They organized a bridal search and found a list of dozen potential suitors. An even bigger dance party would take place and Ouro-Izzaru would pick the smart and courteous Kayjeeka (pronounced "*kejika*") so named because she was born on a *Kayjeeka*, which means "Friday" in the Tem language.

The royal family had now grown to four adult members. This time the king was convinced that the third time would be the charm. Izzaru, Dongoli, Kalama, and Kayjeeka lived together for another three years, still with no child. Worried and frustrated, the king decided to take the matter in his own hands. He knew he was wealthy and surrounded by some of the most powerful healers and oracles ever made. He would take no more advice from anyone, and wouldn't take no for an answer for whatever decision he made.

The king had sworn to sell the last piece of material possession he had, should that be the price to pay to ensure that he have a blood child—preferably a boy to ensure the succession to the throne. All the riches and comfort he was surrounded with failed to make the king a happy man. All the accolades and venerations from across social and political classes were not enough to satisfy the king. One important piece was missing: being a father to the next king. In fact, he was determined to dismantle all those material and immaterial fortunes he had in order to acquire the missing element. Piece by piece, the immense royal fortune was being depleted.

The numerous stocks of gold had now disappeared as he would use them to hire internal and external oracles to help solve his family's fertility problem. Deprived of his gold, the king turned to his massive real estate and that of his subjects who voluntarily obliged. Still no success. Desperate, he then turned to his innumerable herds of livestock, still in vain. Quickly, stocks of farm harvests would follow suit and the results remained the same.

Now he had nothing else to offer, became very poor, and turned the entire kingdom into a miserable and unrecognizable town. Due to the king's personal ambitions, episodic narcissism and selfishness, Lakaza fell from a golden era deeply into a dark abyss in record time. Like a house of cards, piece by piece, the golden kingdom had crumbled before the people's eyes.

Nevertheless, despite losing every material possession he ever had, a few things remained with him and chose to never abandon him: his three wives, his now symbolic throne, his graciousness and legendary hospitality and care for others. The three wives agreed to jointly launch a small trade business. Dongoli, the once rich one, borrowed some money from her siblings to invest in buying and selling used clothes. Kalama, the family-oriented one, would pick the most sellable merchandise for infants, toddlers, and adults. Kayjeeka, the smart and courteous one, was in charge of the tail end of the value chain: retail and customer service. Still, those efforts were not enough to meet the family needs and cater to eventual visitors and guests. On some days, Izzaru and his three wives would starve themselves to ensure that a random visitor had enough to eat. They would beg their subjects for grains in order to feed starving neighbors or unannounced visitors.

Unannounced visits grew more and more frequent as the economic outlook continued to dim across the kingdom. One sunny day in March, a rather unusual one occurred. As the king was preparing to lead his daily cabinet meeting, a lightly dressed and lightly packed stranger knocked at the vestibule door. He seemed rather strong, relatively young, in short not the type of visitors the royal family were used to hosting. He politely asked for temporary shelter at the royal palace, yet deliberately abstained from revealing how long he intended to stay. Out of courtesy and respect for local customs, the hosts opted not to ask, and the guest should feel free to stay as long as he saw fit.

The king instead called up Queen Dongoli and tasked her with being the official host for the guest, making sure he felt welcomed, catered to, and cared for till his departure. Day in and day out, the guest would eat and drink as he needed, while Ouro-Izzaru and his wives settled for forced starvation. Queen Dongoli held her cool for an entire week, and yet the guest gave no sign of being ready to leave.

On the eighth day, Queen Dongoli ran out of cash, out of food, and out of patience. She walked over to her husband and regretfully declared she couldn't take it anymore, and urged the king to send the guest packing. Politely, the guest obliged and left in minutes' notice. For the following few days, Queen

Dongoli worked hard to purchase and sell more merchandise and make up for the financial and material toll she incurred as a result of hosting and feeding the stranger. However, exactly 10 days after the stranger departed, on another sunny day and under similar circumstances, the king was informed of another visitor.

This one looked slightly weaker and in a more dire condition than the previous one. But just like the previous guest, he shared so little about himself and would not reveal where he came from, what specific purpose he was pursuing, nor how long he intended to stay. Without further inquiry, the king called up Queen Kalama and instructed her to make the visitor feel at home and take care of him for the duration of his stay.

"Understood, Ouro. Our illustrious visitor is welcome and should feel at home." Queen Kalama replied with grace and courtesy.

Day in and day out, she would cook for the guest, and not once had he felt hungry while at the palace. Queen Kalama, as usual, went so far as to starve herself and the king to ensure that the guest had enough to eat and drink. On the ninth day she had enough and could not do it anymore. She walked over to her husband and insisted that the guest be asked to go. The king obliged and so did the visitor in minutes' notice. No questions asked.

The royal family then returned to their normal lives, still struggling to make ends meet. However, exactly ten days after this recent departure, another visitor knocked at the palace vestibule door. He looked tired, visibly in need of a rest, and in no mood of much talking. Royal guards brought him to the king, and he officially requested a temporary shelter with not much detail.

Suddenly, the wise king began to notice some unusual patterns with the three visitors. None of them would specify their origin. All of them were particularly taciturn. None of them would specify their departure date. Their visits were each exactly ten days apart, and none of them would give their full identity. The king was puzzled, and yet offered to provide a welcoming environment to the visitor with no further questions asked. This time he called his third wife, Queen Kayjeeka, and asked her to take care of him. The instructions remained the same as before.

"Count on me, Ouro! Welcome to our illustrious visitor!" She replied courteously.

For the following many days, she would cook for him and make sure he had all he needed. A week later, the once tired and shaky visitor regained his strengths and was in a much better shape. The grain stock was once again depleted, yet Queen Kayjeeka wouldn't ask for his departure. Eight days had passed. He was still there. Nine days had passed, and the visitor was still there. Suddenly at twilight of the tenth day, and on his own, the now healthy and stronger visitor freely asked the king to be allowed to leave. He profoundly thanked the entire royal family for their hospitality and offered to return the favor with what he referred to as a "small token."

"Eminent Ouro-Izzaru," he said as he was staring straight inside of his small handbag, "Before I take off, I would like to give you and your family a small token as a sign of gratitude for your legendary hospitality."

"The king's palace is people's palace." Replied the king who remained puzzled by the visitor's demeanor. "You're always welcome here and so is every living person from near and far. Your gift is not required."

"I insist. I came with three companions in my bag, and your hospitality has convinced me that I should give you one of them before I leave as you would be a good host to either one."

"What are those companions? I am intrigued."

"One of them is named *Leedae* (pronounced '*lide*' meaning 'money.') He has the ability to not only restore, but to grow and multiply your lost fortune. The second one is

Luhru (pronounced '*lúrúú*', meaning 'procreation.') This one can fill your house with as many children as you desire. And the third companion is *Sourou* (pronounced '*suru*', meaning 'patience.') He can help with some of your wishes if properly expressed. I refer to all three of them as my Omnipotent Brigade as they have never let me down. Now one of them is yours. Choose carefully."

The King asked for a few minutes so that he could consult with his wives. Consulting advisers—formally or informally—was something relatively new for the king known for his take-no-advice and listen-to-no-one attitude. Clearly the fall from grace had made him a more compromising and humble man.

First, he called up Queen Dongoli and asked her opinion, "So what say you about this? Which of the three would you recommend?"

"I would recommend taking money." She replied. "I mean, think about it. You've lost all of your wealth and we went from the envy of the world to becoming an utter embarrassment in the eyes of our neighbors and the whole kingdom. Money might not make everybody like or respect you, but it sure can afford you a mirror so that you can watch and see who might be plotting to hit you from behind."

"Understood. I'll let you know what I decide to do. In the end, I'm the ultimate decider. You may now leave."

He then sent the royal servant to find Queen Kalama. She ran over and was asked to help pick the best gift.

Her answer was sharp and clear, "I've always been a family person. I was born and raised in a big family, and where I come from children are everything. Children are parents' best mirror in life. Through children's eyes, parents reflect their worldview, through children's mouths, parents express their successes and shortcomings to humanity, and through children's pocket sizes, parents project their parenting successes and failures. I would advise that you choose Luhru. She will lead us to everything else we wish for."

"Understood. I'll let you know what I decide to do. In the end, I'm the ultimate decider. You may now leave." He replied.

Lastly, he invited the Queen Kayjeeka over with the same question.

She took a deep breath, pondered for some time, analyzed all the options, and then replied, "You remember when you used to be rich? You remember when you lost all your money and every material possession in pursuit of procreation? You remember the only things that stuck with you through thick and thin?

"It's been your three wives. You know the glue that has stuck them to your house? It's patience. You remember the visitation test these three rather odd visitors have put us through over the past few weeks? It's to gauge our common patience in tolerating their presence. Eventually, after two unsuccessful attempts, we've passed the first step on the third try. Let's not blow this last step. Patience has kept us together, and only she could help us move out of this predicament."

"Understood. I'll let you know what I decide to do. In the end, I'm the ultimate decider. You may now leave." He replied and asked the servant to bring back the visitor into the meeting room.

"I have analyzed all of your options, and I've decided to go with Sourou. She has supported us from distance in the past, and we'll be honored to keep her for good."

Without a single word, the visitor pulled *Sourou* (patience) out of his handbag, handed it over to King Izzaru, closed back the handbag, put it back on his right shoulder, and prepared to take off. However, no sooner did he turn to go than the two remaining companions in the handbag began to argue violently.

"Of the two of us, I'm the most desired one because I can multiply and perpetuate humanity." said *Luhru* (procreation) out loud, so loud that even outsiders could understand.

"You're so jealous because everybody likes me. Old, young, men, women, and even children cherish me. They're nothing without me, and I alone can provide everything else and address human needs." *Leedae* (money) retorted.

Realizing that they were being too loud and listened to, the two companions suddenly lowered their voices and began to speak in a calmer manner. After a moment of two-party deliberations, Leedae had made up his mind.

"We've been together for a very long time. In the past, every time we would argue, Sourou would step in and reason with us. Why don't we run to her so that she can help us solve this once and for all?"

Leedae and Luhru slowly and gently slid out of the handbag, running to Sourou for the best advice.

"You have a valid point, dear Leedae." Sourou turned to Leedae. "Without you, we would all starve and stay homeless."

"You're making a valid point too, my dear Luhru. Without you, humanity is doomed to extinction. You are both important in your own ways."

After pondering for a moment, Leedae turned to Luhru and with a more resigned tone, "For as long as we have been together, never have we yelled at each other in this manner. You know why? Because Sourou was with us and has always been the voice of reason. I can't envision life without her, and thus I'm staying with her."

"I think you're right. Without Sourou, I can't visualize what my life will be like, especially with you around." Luhru replied. "I owe my millennia-long survival to her, and I'll dedicate the remainder of my life to her."

The three companions jumped into each other's arms and walked happily into the royal palace. Before he left, the visitor murmured a few last words to the king.

"I've been with them for long enough to understand them. Sourou is the glue that has held them together. Of the three, Sourou is the one who deliberately avoids jumping on burning plates, but rather waits for the food to cool down before eating, for better taste and fewer accidents. You and your family have nurtured patience for so long. Your food is now cool enough and you may eat it.

"Wisdom is what differentiates good leaders from bad ones. Socioeconomic conditions are merely ephemeral. Even while being infertile and bearing no children, a great king never loses his crown. Let it be known that your wisdom has reopened the way back to your once lost opulence. Your ability to hold on to Sourou will determine its duration."

Ever since that day, the Palace recovered and surpassed its once respected and envied stature. King Izzaru and his three wives made tens of children and the entire progeny grew to restore dignity and respect for the Kingdom. Before he died, King Izzaru made his children promise to erect a gold-plated monument in honor of the three inseparable companions. His children went even farther by renaming the Kingdom *Souroudè*, (pronounced "*surudɛ*") translated literally as "Home of Patience."

The Birth Of Fire – South Africa

Narrated by Zodwa Dorcas Ndlela

Translated by Sipho C. Ndlela, PhD

A fable from the Zulu tribe

Kwasukasukela (once a upon a time), animals roamed freely and peacefully in a world where they had everything they desired, except for one thing: warmth at night. The days were hot. However, when night fell, cold pierced the skins of the animals in this kingdom and left them miserable.

One day, the King of the land, *Indlovu* (the Elephant), had a bright idea. "What if I asked the sun to never go to sleep?"

Having thought that, he looked up the sky and began trumpeting, which echoed every corner of his kingdom. *Sun, hear my call, never sleep, your glow is life to this kingdom.* Indlovu repeated from sunrise to sunset, but the sun never heard his call.

Drained and exhausted, the Indlovu waited for another day. This time, he gathered all animals, from all corners of his Kingdom.

"Today, I need a strong animal that can run to the end of this Kingdom, chase the sun, day and night, and ask for the sun to always stay up to give us warmth."

All animals looked around, thinking, *Who could that be!*

With no hesitation, the Eagle, perched high up, shouted, "My King, I am ready to serve you, allow me to fulfill your wish."

The elephant responded, "Eagle, this is no bird's duty. He needs a strong, muscular animal that can run."

Indlovu gathered all animals from all corners of his Kingdom

All animals kept quiet, now wondering again, who that animal could be. Soon, the King, called for the *Inyamazane* (deer or springbok).

Excited, Indlovu said, "I choose you to go and ask the sun, never to sleep."

Without hesitation, the Inyamazane, took off, ran day and night in search for the sun's destiny, but never caught it. Tired, and cold at night, he came back exhausted, with no good news. Soon the elephant asked loudly for another strong muscular, runner, that can see in the dark.

Without hesitation, the eagle, responded, "King, I am ready to serve you."

Annoyed, the Elephant responded, "This is no bird's duty."

This time, the King chose the *Ingwe* (Leopard). "You, run till the end of this Kingdom. Ask the sun to never sleep."

The journey began. Ingwe ran day and night with no luck at meeting the sun, returning home tired. The King wasn't ready to give up and summoned the animals for another stronger, fast runner.

Again, the Eagle, without giving up, said, "My King, let me serve you!"

The King had a change of heart and agreed. Joyfully, the Eagle, jumped and open it wings flew straight up, while all animals gazed in surprise.

The Eagle was so strong, he reached the sun and asked for one thing, "Never sleep. Our Kingdom needs your warmth."

The Sun, being generous, gave the Eagle a beautiful glowing crystal and placed it into its paws. "This is for you and the whole Kingdom. I cannot always serve you because I also get tired and need to sleep too. Take this crystal and share it with the kingdom."

With joy, the Eagle flew back home. As it approached, all animals could see the glowing crystal and wondered what it was. As promised, the Eagle delivered the message to Indlovu from the Sun. Indlovu then gave all animals a small piece of the glowing crystal to always keep with them and use during night fall. The animals never felt cold again. The magical crystal ball was the fire that we see today. From then onward, the Eagle became the King of the Sky.

Tsuro na Gudo (Hare and Baboon) – Zimbabwe

By Thamba Tabvuma

A fable from the Shona tribe

Way, way back in time, when donkeys still had horns as large as kudu horns, when rock rabbits had tails like monkeys, when flies were sacred and would climb mountains, there were two boys named *Tsuro na Gudo* (hare and baboon.) Tsuro called Gudo *sekuru* since his mother was the sister to Gudo's father. Now because these two were very similar in age, they had a tight and close relationship like a belt and its trousers—inseparable. Tired of eating wild gooseberries at home, they ran away to their hideout in the forest.

Over the first few days, they would survive on what Gudo would manage to steal from the surrounding farms, and Tsuro would do the cooking. As one with a gift of using his head, Tsuro began to think up a plan to get delicacies like meat and milk.

Early one morning he woke up and said to Gudo, "Sekuru, the desire for meat is truly making me sick right now. I have thought to go to the people on the other side of the mountain and take their meat. Thereafter I want to milk the cows at the farm that we saw yesterday because I also have a deep craving for milk right now."

"Are you losing your mind, my cousin?" Gudo quickly answered, feeling sorry for Tsuro. "How will you do things that only dogs are capable of doing?"

"Well, leave that to me cousin." Tsuro swiftly rose and left Gudo looking perplexed.

Tsuro then left their hiding place as the sun was setting, knowing that this was the time that people would be headed home. Upon seeing the people headed down the road from a distance, Tsuro went and lay down on the road and pretended to be dead. After some time had passed, Tsuro heard the ox wagon drawing closer, filled with sacks of meat.

In his heart he prayed, "My ancestors, please see me."

A boy around the age of thirteen was leading the wagon as it arrived where Tsuro lay. When the boy saw Tsuro, he immediately stopped the wagon and said to the older brother who was with him,

"Brother, I have just picked up this rabbit. Its body is still warm. I think someone hit it with a club and it ran and died here."

The brother took Tsuro and threw him into the back of the wagon with the other sacks of meat. This just put the biggest little smirk on Tsuro's face since he was now the ant in the sugar bowl. Tsuro quickly threw out five sacks of meat then jumped out before anyone had seen him. He then ran with great haste to get Gudo to help him carry the sacks to the hideout. Gudo was stunned by what he saw.

"How did you come across all this meat, cousin?"

"These fists, Gudo. The way I beat those people was just terrible. My hands are burdened with pain. I stopped the ox wagon then started dishing it out to the boy. He was too stunned to even cry. The sent a dog out, so I used my strong right foot and that was that. That is when I said to the big brother, 'You, over there, take down three of those sacks for me and I'll be on my way.' When he tried to protest, I unleashed my fists with such great fury that instead of releasing three sacks, I saw that he did me a favor and gave me five."

Upon hearing this, Gudo's heart sank and he couldn't help but wonder to himself, "How can this be? I am too big and strong to be overshadowed by my little cousin."

From the time Tsuro told him his incredible tale, Gudo had a heavy heart. He was behaving like a possessed beast. Sleep had found another home. When he managed to catch some he would dream he was delivering such great blows that when he ordered them to give him the meat, they would give him way more than Tsuro's.

Whenever he got a chance, he would practice a punching routine specifically targeting the jawline. He would pull out shrubs and bushes and use them for practice mastering his jabs and kicks. He would bob and weave under overhanging tree branches and be quick to dispense a straight left to an offending leaf. Gudo was preparing for the battle of his life. He had eaten fruit from the tree of anarchy.

With a ferociousness second to none, Gudo clobbered through the meat Tsuro had taken, believing that his courage would be realized when the bounty arrived. The next morning he woke up having fallen from the high table. The time he had been waiting for had come. With his heart set, he went for the hunters. He believed in his strength. He hadn't thought through any other plan that did not involve his fists.

As they came down the road, Gudo came out of the thick onto the road, stood in front of the ox wagon, and said, "Ho! Ho!"

Just then, they heard baboons shout out in the forest. He went ahead and dished a big slap to the young boy at the head of the wagon. Then he added a right boot to cement the message. The boy started to cry.

"Keep quiet. Stop distressing. I haven't even started yet. You will see what I will do to your big brother. I'll give him one that will rearrange his teeth. What Tsuro did to you all will pale in comparison to what I will do to you today."

Seeing that his younger brother might get hurt, the older brother called to him. "Run towards me. This baboon looks like he has the crazy in him."

The baboon did not like hearing this at all. The anger in him rose.

"You, who are you saying is crazy!" he shouted at the brother. "Buffoon. You idiot that eats soil! Today you shall see me! You will know why dogs cannot laugh! Beware, I'm warning you!"

The brother was an accomplished hunter and well versed in the pugilistic arts, unbeknown to Gudo. They approached each other, staring each other down with venom in their eyes. Gudo unleashed his well-practiced right hook. The brother ducked the blow easily, then finding his balance released a haymaker of his own, landing it squarely on Gudo's jaw. Down the baboon went. Suddenly realizing that his fists of fury might not be up to the challenge, he thought he would resort to biting him with his large teeth.

As he was going to bite, he heard, "Ruff, Ruff!"

Suddenly he realized there was Bingo and Ringo ready to tear into him

Suddenly he realized there was Bingo and Ringo ready to tear into him. Due to his lack of planning, dogs hadn't even crossed his mind. Truth be told, Gudo feared dogs as much as he did lions.

"My gods, what I have eaten has risen." He prayed, his heart in his mouth.

Drawing all the strength he had, he said, "Do you still love these dogs? If you have any love for them, hold them back. You boy, come here and hold these beasts. You brother, unload all those sacks off the wagon and put them over there! Do you hear what I am?"

He did not get a chance to finish. Ringo had got a good bite of his leg.

"Oh my, oh my! Ahhh!" Gudo yelled.

He lashed out, giving the dog a big slap. Ringo gave out a cry but resumed his business on the leg. Gudo's confidence rose. He launched an all-out attack on the dog. Bingo joined the fight by going straight in and biting Gudo's tail. The battle had begun in earnest. The brother meanwhile grabbed his club and started pounding on Gudo's back. The baboon slouched his back in pain. Till today, baboons walk with a slouch in their back because of this.

Gudo ran, praying his feet would carry him. The dogs tried to give chase but threw their spears down, for the baboon had made friends with the wind. When he had made it to small hill, he started throwing stones at Bingo and Ringo till they ran back to their master. Because of his hunger, Gudo started eating insects from under the rocks. Till this day, baboons continue to eat insects they find from under the rocks.

"So it is Tsuro that has made me get into all this trouble today." Gudo said to himself shortly after. "Today I shall confront him. I cannot deny my mother's ancestors who stripped the back off beasts. Today he will regret the day he was born."

He then started his journey back to the hideout where Tsuro was waiting.

The Magic Seeds – Angola

by Yola Castro and John Bella
Translation by Yuri Santos
A fable from the Bangala tribe

Many, many years ago in a village in downtown *Cassange* in the province of *Malanje*, there was a soba (traditional authority) named José. José was known for having lots of land and being kind to the people of his tribe. He lived with two grandchildren and a pet called Pimba, who always kept them safe. His granddaughter, Ginga, was docile and affectionate and always stood by her grandfather. Dudu, his grandson, was like his sister, but he dreamed of wealth and power.

This story was told by a soba of a *Bangala Tribe* (a tribe from the Lunda Norte Province of Angola) so that his children, grandchildren, and the generations beyond from that region would keep the moral teachings of the lesson. Until this date, the story is still shared amongst the villages. The story goes:

"My dear grandchildren, I am about to die, I have an incurable disease. The *curandeiro* (traditional healer) gave me just two days and two nights to live," said the soba.

"The time has come to say: you are my greatest treasure, but I only have two magic seeds and our mascot, Pimba, to leave you as an inheritance."

"Seeds? Seeds, grandpa? What shall we do with seeds? And with the pet?" said Dudu.

*I only have two magic seeds and our mascot, Pimba,
to leave you as an inheritance*

Ginga replied, "My brother, let our grandfather speak. Can't you see he can't speak? Have patience and we will listen to you!"

The grandfather responded, "Don't be angry, my friend and faithful friend Pimba. I'll leave you nothing. I'll just ask you to continue to protect my grandchildren as you always did.

"Here are my relics I have kept for many years to give you as an inheritance. From the moment that each one receives these seeds, you can do with them what you want. When you think it's time to organize your lives without me, and you need a lot of help, just rub the seeds with both hands, until they warm up and make an upward gesture.

"Any request you make shall be granted to you. However, beware! You must be intelligent, very intelligent, not to regret your decisions."

A new day dawned. Ginga was so sad, that she didn't notice the sun shone like never before but for her everything was dark and boring. She knew she was going to lose her grandfather soon. She cried and lamented.

From that moment, everything had lost its colors. She loved to see the rooster crowing, the birds in the mulberry trees, the *cabiocotos* (caterpillars) that ate the new leaves of the plants. Nothing more made sense.

On the other hand, Dudu jumped with joy because of the luck he expected. He dreamed of being very rich, having lots of farmland, cattle, and people working for him. He did not hesitate to take his magic seed, pack his bag and put it on his back in search of the best place in downtown *Cassange* (a district in Malanje).

"My friend Pimba, I need your help," said Gugu. "Dudu left me alone. You are the only one who can help me. You have known me since I was born. I have no one else in the family to support me. I will need you a lot. I need advice. Can you give it to me?"

"My dear girl, advice is not with me," responded Pimba. "I will defend you tooth and nail. I can save you from the water and my wild companions, but advice? Um…I only know a wise woman capable of giving you advice—the Master Tamara! But to talk to her, we will have to travel. We have a long way to go. Are you willing to go on a trip, right now? Do you have the courage?"

And so they went at full speed and without resting. They crossed valleys and mountains, lakes and ponds, jumped from vine to vine, taking shortcuts along the way and picking up speed. They traveled a full day and night without getting tired until they found a creek.

Ginga sat on the first place she found while Pimba was enjoying the beautiful landscape. In the middle of the buzz from the water stream that flowed there, both heard a calm voice, but very sonorous that was heard saying, "Ai ai ai ai ai."

"Would you mind coming out on top of me, please?" asked Master Tamara. "I need to move."

"My sincere apologies, Master Tamara," replied Ginga. "I was so tired that I sat in the first place I saw and it was you. I'm sorry."

"Master Tamara, this girl is the granddaughter of Soba José," said Pimba. "I brought her because she needs your advice."

"Are you granddaughter of José the Soba?" asked Mestre Tamara. "Tell me why you are looking for me. How can I help you?"

Ginga spent hours telling Master Tamara about her grandfather. She told her how Grandpa José is so supportive of his community and how much he cared and loved his grandchildren. Ginga cried at the thought of what the community would be like without their soba and how she would live without the love of her beloved grandfather. Ginga cried, begging Master Tamara to do something for her. Then Master Tamara finally spoke.

She said, "In the face of so much loving gestures to your grandfather and neighbors, I will do everything to help you my dear friend. But I cannot do anything now. My magic portions are a day and night away from here and I fear that one day and night will be too late to help you."

"My grandfather said that in a time of great need, these seeds would help me. Maybe I can help you and me," replied Ginga.

"How wonderful!" said Master Tamara. "I see that your grandfather kept the two seeds that I gave him. And I see that you did not waste your seed with materialism or superfluous things. This changes everything, my girl. We just need to wait for nightfall and climb to the top of the mountain. Let's make the magic happen!"

Then the night came. On the top of the mountain and under the moonlight and stars, Master Tamara said her wise words and sang her magic song.

Master Tamara asked Ginga to make her wish using her magic seeds. Remembering her grandfather's words, she rubs her seed with both hands until she warms it up, and then gestures upwards and then the magic began to happen. The seed, listening the desire of Ginga's mind, begun to shine and became a great and magnificent star.

"You are very smart, Ginga ," acknowledged Master Tamara. "You are a beautiful and wise girl with a very kind heart.

Now go back home and you will see what awaits you."

Ginga and Pimba immediately following Tamara's advice. They traveled another night and another day to return to the Soba´s village. Upon arrival, Ginga found her grandfather healthy as he hadn't seen him in a while. He embraced her like he would never let go again.

Ginga noticed everything had changed. The village had become more beautiful and greener, a square was born close to the village supplying the region with water and fish. Everything was perfect except for Dudu, who had never been reached out since his journey for power and fortune.

Months later, to the delight of the family, Dudu returned home, crestfallen, sad and hungry. The family didn't hesitate to embrace Dudu with love and warmth, but they were curious about what happened to him in the time during the period he left without giving news.

Later Dudu explained that the same day he traveled, he rubbed his magic seed and made his request and then buried the seed, waiting for dawn. At dawn, a farm sprang from their desires, and peasants looking for work.

The farm brought wealth and power to Dudu. It also brought him arrogance. He did not speak to his workers without shouting, always suspicious and authoritarian. Two of his best peasants, named Turbão and Bangão, shared the same ambitions as Dudu.

The more authoritarian and arrogant Dudu became, the greater was the urge for Turbão and Bangão to do something about it. They discovered that Dudu's weak point was gambling. They convinced Dudu to bet all of his wealth and farm on a game and he lost. Losing everything made Dudu realize what was important to him: his family.

Dudu promised to never repeat his acts and to be more friendly to family. And do everything to be respected by his tribe and his grandfather. Dudu kept his promises. They lived happily together for generations and generations.

This story teaches us that our parents are our foundation. It is our duty to care for them better than anyone else. Material things are useful but we must not be greedy. We conquer material things but in difficult times we need to help those in need. Above all, we need to learn how to use the great gift that God has given us — our intelligence.

The Broken Spoon – Cameroon

By Nina Taka

A fable from the Bamileke tribe

This is the story of a little boy called Wanji, who lived with his father, Tanyi, and his stepmother, Meh'kheu, in a village beyond the mighty forest and the seven rivers. Meh'kheu had a daughter called Mohmeh. She was Wanji's half-sister. Tanyi had wedded Meh'Kheu after Wanji's mother died during childbirth.

Wanji longed for his mother every day because Meh'kheu made his life miserable in every possible way. His stepmother, Meh'kheu didn't like him. She always made him do all the difficult chores at home and was quick to reprimand him.

One day, Meh'kheu told Wanji to go to the river and wash the dishes. Wanji did as he was told, and as he washed the dishes, he broke a spoon. Paralyzed with fear, he began to cry, for he knew what to expect when he returned home. When he got home, he told Meh'kheu that he had broken a spoon. Furious, Meh'kheu sent Wanji out of the house telling him to come back once he had a new spoon to replace the broken one.

The boy left the house without water, without food, and without knowing where he should go. He crossed the seven rivers and walked into the mighty forest for many days and many nights, eating only what he could find, hardly sleeping. One day, as he walked, he saw a house in the distance, nestled in the forest and decided to go there. As he entered, he saw a dirty old woman. He greeted her softly, and asked her if she had a place for him to rest.

The old lady looked surprised. She said, "What brings you here, my boy?"

Wanji began to weep and told him of the story of how he had broken his stepmother's spoon and how she had asked him not to return until he found a new one.

"Don't cry little one." the old woman told Wanji. "Calm down, have some food and rest. You are very tired and need to gain some strength."

Wanji did as he was told, the following morning, just as the birds began to sing, signaling the birth of a new day, Wanji woke up.

He went to the old woman, who sat by the fire in her kitchen, smoking what looked like an ancient pipe. Her skin was soft and flabby, with deep wrinkles everywhere, but her face bore the marks of wisdom and compassion.

Moved by her gentle presence, Wanji asked her,

"Grandmother, can I go to the river to fetch you some water to drink? You have been very kind to me."

The old lady said yes and handed him a calabash to fetch water from the river. Wanji returned with the calabash full of water. He made sure to sweep the old woman's house, cooked her some food, and washed her feet.

At noon, when the sun stood firm in the sky, he went to the old woman and said,

"Grandmother, it is time for me to leave. I need to find a new spoon for my stepmother."

The old woman listened to him attentively. "You see my little one." she said to him,

"Here you are going in search of a spoon. Listen carefully to what I'm going to tell you. When you walk, at a certain point, you will see six balls on the ground, all extremely fragile. You shouldn't be afraid. The first three will say to you, 'Take us, take us," and the other three will say to you, 'Do not take us, do not take us.' Take the last three. Do you understand?"

Wanji answered with a silent nod, and with a heavy heart, he bid the old woman farewell, and resumed his journey through the forest.

He walked for many days and many nights, eating what he could find, sleeping very little. In his heart of hearts, he longed for his mother.

One day, as he walked wearily, all of a sudden, he saw six balls lined up in front of him.

Three of them shouted, "Take us, take us."

The other three shouted, "Don't take us, don't take us."

As soon as he heard them, he remembered the old lady's words to him. He stopped by the balls that shouted, "Don't take us," picked them up, and travelled on with them. He walked for many days and many nights, eating what he could find, sleeping very little. In his heart of hearts, he longed for his mother.

All of a sudden, he saw six balls lined up in front of him

One day, recalling what the old woman had said, he broke the first ball. Out of it appeared weapons of all sorts, akin to those of a king fully armored and ready for war. He broke the second ball. A host of wild animals appeared from the forest ready to devour him. Without thinking, he killed them with the weapons from the previous ball. He then decided to break the last ball and to his great surprise, he saw a large and beautiful house in which were the loveliest golden spoons he had ever seen.

He picked one of them and made his way back to his village, his heart full of joy and gratitude to the old woman who had given him precious guidance.

He walked through the mighty forest and crossed the seven rivers back to his father's house and went to Meh'kheu, his stepmother.

He said, "Dear stepmother, this is the spoon you asked me to find and bring back to you."

Meh'kheu was surprised for she believed the boy had died. Who could survive alone through the mighty forest and the seven rivers, let alone a boy? She gasped in astonishment when she saw the golden spoon that the boy Wanji laid in her hands. It was the finest thing she had ever seen. She was overcome with envy. She called her own daughter, Mohmeh, and sent her to the river to wash the dishes, telling her make sure she came back with a broken spoon.

Mohmeh did as her mom told her, she went to the river to do the dishes, broke a spoon, came home, and told her mom that a spoon was broken. Her mother instantly chased her out of the house, asking her not to come back until she found a new spoon.

Like the boy, Mohmeh crossed the seven rivers and walked into the mighty forest for many hours and many nights. Suddenly she saw the house the boy had seen. She went there and saw the same old lady. Unlike Wanji, Mohmeh despised the old lady! She did not deign to greet the old lady because she was dirty and smelled bad. Haughtily, she asked the old lady why she was so dirty.

The lady did not answer the question, but wanted to offer Mohmeh hospitality. Mohmeh refused and decided to leave immediately. The old lady nevertheless gave her the same advice as the boy. She told her about the six balls she would meet, and told her which ones she should take and which she should not take.

But the little girl thought the old woman was stupid. After all, what could a dirty, stinky old woman know? She resumed her journey and did as she saw fit. She walked for many nights and many days, until one day she saw six balls on her path. She stooped and picked the balls that said, "Take us."

She broke the first ball and instantly wild animals from the forest pounced on her and killed her.

Meh'kheu waited in vain for Mohmeh, her little girl. Several years passed but Mohmeh for years and never returned. Ashamed, she went to the boy and asked him how he had managed to find the golden spoon. With his usual candour, and not knowing that this stepmother had also sent his stepsister in search of a spoon, Wanji told her his whole story. Meh'kheu, humiliated and bitter, fell down and wept. She was inconsolable for the rest of her life. As for the boy, he married, formed a very large family and took care of his father, Tanyi, in spite of everything.

The Legend Of Sinimory – Cote d'Ivoire

By Ousmane Diallo, PhD

A fable from the Wassoulou people of the Mandingo tribe

Once upon a time, in the depths of the Mandingo land, there was a small village where the inhabitants lived peacefully. It was the time where some animals were still able to talk to humans. In that village there was an old man who married a wicked woman in his second marriage. This woman did not like the two sons of the first wife who had been dead for several years. She reserved the hardest work for Maméry and Sinimory, while her sons Mamadou and Samba spent their time playing all day in the dust. Fortunately, not all stepmothers are mean and evil like this woman.

The old man was tired and could no longer go to the farm or plow the family's field. Early every morning, Maméry and Sinimory went to the field to clear the ground. They fed themselves with wild fruits and roots. At night they came home very tired.

"You're very dirty," the stepmother said. "Go wash at the river. I don't have enough water for you."

Before the two children returned, she served the evening meal to Mamadou and Samba. Sinimory and his brother often went to sleep on an empty stomach.

One day, Maméry, the eldest, said to Sinimory, "Listen, Sinimory, I can no longer bear this suffering. I've had enough. I want to go. Come with me."

"Brother, but what will become of our father without us?" Sinimory asked. "Mamadou and Samba never learned to cultivate the land. This heartless woman will let him starve. Think of our father and stay with him."

"Stay here if you want. I have to go." Then Maméry went away, leaving his brother alone with his father.

After Maméry left, the stepmother brought Sinimory in and said, "You should have left with your brother. If you stayed here, it's surely because you want your father's inheritance. I'm telling you, Sinimory, you'll never get it. There is barely enough wealth for me and my two sons."

"It's because of my father that I stay here," replied Sinimory. "He is very old and can no longer bear the work of the fields. What would he do without me?"

Sinimory thus continued his life with only Labou, his faithful dog. Labou spoke like men when he was alone with Sinimory.

The stepmother had bad intentions. *I have to remove Sinimory,* she thought to herself, *So my two sons Mamadou and Samba will be happy.*

Being so evil, she had forbidden Labou from following Sinimory to the field after his brother left. She wanted him to be lonely, and in case he got bitten by a snake, he would have no one to alert the villagers for assistance and would die.

The wicked stepmother went from village to village to visit the most feared witches, to acquire the deadliest poison in order to kill Sinimory.

One evening she said, "Sinimory, you are a brave child. I've always been mean to you. Please forgive me. From now on, I will cook and take the food to you every day so you will not have to eat wild fruits and roots for lunch.

After all, you are the one who grow these foods."

Surprised by his stepmother's offer, he could only wonder what her motivations were. Sinimory then told Labou about his stepmother's offer, and that he did not trust her.

The next day, before going to the field, Sinimory said to his dog, "Take a good look at what's going on. If you see anything, come and let me know."

During the day, the stepmother prepared rice, yam and sweet potatoes. She put poison in the rice and sweet potato dish. The little dog that was watching all this ran to warn his master and sang this song:

"Sinimory, Oh!
Sinimory, my master,
If your stepmother gives you a plate of rice, do not eat it.
Refuse it, Sinimory, because this dish contains poison.

If your stepmother gives you a plate of sweet potatoes,

Refuse to eat it, Sinimory, because this dish also contains poison.

But if she gives you yams, eat them, eat them, Sinimory.

The yam dish does not contain any poison.

And on the day I won't be there to warn you, Sinimory.

The day I will be killed, Sinimory,

Go far from here, Sinimory.

Otherwise the land you clear will eat you."

When the step mother arrived with the dishes, Sinimory ate only yams. *This Sinimory is a sorcerer,* thought the stepmother. *How could he have guessed?*

The next day the stepmother prepared a dish of *fonio* (a type of millet) and a meat dish. She put poison in the meat dish. Labou, the little dog, ran to prevent his master from eating the poisoned dish.

"Sinimory Oh!

Sinimory, my master.

If your stepmother gives you a plate of meat, refuse it.

Refuse it, Sinimory, because this dish contains poison.

If she presents you with a fonio *dish, eat it.*

Eat it, Sinimory.

The fonio *dish does not contain any poison.*

And on the day, I won't be there to warn you, Sinimory.

The day I will be killed Sinimory,

Go far from here, Sinimory.

Otherwise the land you clear will eat you."

That day, Sinimory ate *fonio* and refused the meat.

"How did he know?" the stepmother said to herself. "We'll see what happens tomorrow."

The next day, she prepared several dishes. She locked herself in her room and put the poison in one of them. She then opened the door and continued her cleaning. Labou then approached the dishes, and sniffed them one by one to find out which contained the poison.

The stepmother surprised him and said, "Ah! It's you, you filthy beast, who warns Sinimory every time of what I do. Today, you're not going to tell anyone what you saw."

At these words, the stepmother picked up a piece of wood and killed the little dog.

Sinimory waited till almost the time his wicked stepmother usually arrived, without seeing his faithful friend, Labou come. Not seeing him arrive, he remembered Labou's song:

"On the day, I won't be there to warn you, Sinimory.
The day I will be killed, Sinimory,
Go far from here, Sinimory.

Otherwise the land you clear will eat you."

With those thoughts, Sinimory left. He walked for days, weeks, months. He crossed mountains and rivers, forests and savannahs. He always fed on wild fruits and roots. In the evening, he would climb the trees and sleep there.

One morning when he woke up, he saw two snakes fighting at the foot of a tree. The victor of the fight took a leaf and put it on the head of the other snake. He regained consciousness and the two snakes continued their fight while moving away. Sinimory descended from the tree, observed the leaf at length, and then went away.

After hours of walking, he climbed a tree to rest. Suddenly, he saw an owl flying towards him and an eagle chasing him. Sinimory broke a branch and felled the eagle with a blow.

"Thank you, handsome young man," said the owl. "What is your name?"

"My name is Sinimory," answered the boy.

"Thank you very much for saving my life. I'll give you a secret; it'll be your reward. Look at that tree. If you pour a few drops of the sap of this tree into the eyes of a blind person, he or she will regain their sight."

Sinimory thanked his new friend and continued his walk.

The next day at noon, Sinimory arrived in a clearing where he surprised a group of gorillas sitting in circles.

"Who are you, and what are you doing here?" asked the head of the gorillas.

Sinimory told his story.

"Come to me," said the gorilla. "Wash yourself with this water and drink some."

After the bath, the head of the gorillas said to him, "From today on, no spear and no bullet will be able to pierce your body. Even the poison won't hurt you anymore."

After thanking and then greeting the leader of the gorillas, Sinimory went back on the road again. After a several hours he arrived in a big town.

"What's going on here?" said Sinimory to a passerby. "Why are you all so sad?"

"Stranger," answered the old man, "Our king's only daughter died this morning. A snake bit her while she was playing with her friends in the royal garden."

"And no one could save her?" asked the young Sinimory.

"Nobody. She will be buried tomorrow."

Sinimory remembered the battle between the two snakes. Determined to help the people of this town, Sinimory returned to the place of the fight and picked the magic leaves.

He rushed back to the big town, and announced to the old man, "Take me to the king. I can help him save his beloved daughter."

"What are you doing at my house?" the king asked Sinimory. "Can't you see that I am mourning?"

"I would like to see the princess and try to bring her back to life."

"I thank you, Sinimory, but what can a young man like you do? My greatest healers have not succeeded."

Sinimory insisted so much that the king led him to the princess' body. Sinimory pressed the leaves into a calabash and added water. He dripped that juice into the princess's nostrils. She opened her eyes and said,

"What's going on father? Did I get too much sleep?"

The king hugged his daughter and shed tears of joy. "You are the strongest healer, Sinimory. Ask me anything you want and I'll give it to you. My greatest reward is resuscitating your daughter. But, if I could settle in your kingdom..."

The king built a beautiful house for Sinimory and gave him a hundred cows, a hundred sheep, a hundred camels, a hundred chickens, a hundred cases of gold, and a hundred servants. He also gave him vast fields of millet, rice, and yams. He gave him clothes embroidered with gold.

"I also offer you the most beautiful horse of my kingdom." said the king.

The news of Princess Nagnouma's return to life and the feat of Sinimory crossed the borders of the kingdom. All the princes of the neighboring regions came to ask the king for the hand of Princess Nagnouma. They all brought beautiful gifts for the princess.

The king announced, "I only have one daughter. Who am I going to give her hand to?"

Turning back to Sinimory, he went on, "You, Sinimory, who revived my daughter, you must help me. Find a solution to this problem."

"O my king, organize a fight and give your daughter to the victor. Thus, the princess will always be protected by a brave soldier."

"Thank you Sinimory. You are young, but you know a lot of things. From now on you will live near me, to advise me."

The fight was announced in all neighboring villages and tribes. Even the old Sigui, the great sorcerer, presented himself. The big day came. The candidates faced off each other two by two. The weakest ones were defeated by the strongest. The evening came and there were only two fighters left: the king Dato and the old Sigui.

Princess Nagnoma then looked at the king Dato and the old Sigui and said to herself, "The king Dato is a valiant warrior but he is ugly. As for Sigui, he's old and not the right husband for a young lady like me."

Turning towards Sinimory, the young princess said to him, "Sinimory, you saved my life before. You have to help me again."

"I cannot fight for you, pretty princess. I am neither a prince nor a king."

"I would rather die than be the wife of one of these two kings."

Dato and Sigui clashed and Dato won.

"I am the winner," Dato said. "Tomorrow, as soon as the sun rises, I will return to my kingdom with the most beautiful of princesses."

"I won't go with you tomorrow. I need a few days to get ready."

"I'll be waiting for you, Nagnouma. Don't forget that you now belong to king Dato."

Sigui then approached the princess. "I'm old, it's true. But I'm telling you, Nagnouma, Dato will never have you."

Sigui then took out of his pocket a white powder which he threw at the figure of the pretty princess, who immediately went blind.

"I can't see anymore," cried the pretty princess. "Sigui made me blind."

"On guard, Sigui!" shouted Dato. "You blinded my fiancée."

The fight resumed. It lasted a long time. Blood flowed, and for the second time, Dato won.

"My daughter belongs to you, Dato" the king told him. "You just proved that you are the only one who deserves Nagnouma. You can take her whenever you want."

"What would I do with a blind princess?" asked Dato. "Give your daughter to another prince. I don't want her anymore."

All the princes, in turn, refused the blind princess. The king announced that he would give his daughter in marriage to the one who would restore her sight. Healers arrived from all corners of the kingdom. No one could cure her.

"Sinimory," said the king, "You saved my daughter from death. Can you restore her sight? If you can cure her, you will be king after me."

"I love Princess Nagnouma," said Sinimory. "I will try to get her sight back."

Sinimory remember what the owl said to him, "If you pour a few drops of the sap from this tree into the eyes of a blind man, he will regain his sight."

Sinimory went to collect a few drops of this sap. On his return, he met the old man who had taken him to the king when he first arrived in the kingdom.

"Sinimory, I recognize you," said the old man. "You are the one who saved the princess."

"The princess is still alive," replied Sinimory. "But Sigui made her blind. I want to help her a second time."

"Can I go with you?" asked the old man.

Sinimory agreed and both men went to the palace. When they got to the princess, Sinimory placed a few drops of sap into her eyes. Immediately the pretty princess exclaimed,

"I see, I see! I have regained my sight!"

She then threw herself into her father's arms.

"Sinimory," announced the king," I give you my daughter in marriage. When I die, you'll be king. With your wisdom, you will understand and help the inhabitants of my kingdom."

Turning to his people, the king continued, "When the moon is on the fourteenth day of its race, Sinimory and my daughter will get married."

The wedding day arrived. People came from all parts of the kingdom to attend the festival. Sinimory was dressed like a king. Suddenly the princess appeared. Her head was covered in jewels and gold. A white veil covered her face. The women who accompanied her sang.

"Oh, how beautiful she is," some said.

"She is the prettiest princess of all kingdoms," said the others.

The traditional dances followed the wedding ceremony.

Sinimory was dressed like a king and the princess was covered in jewels and gold

In the middle of the dance, someone suddenly came in and shouted, "It's me, Dato. I am here to pick up my wife."

"My daughter is now the wife of Sinimory," replied the king.

"I refused to take your daughter as a wife because she was blind," said Dato. "Since she has regained her sight, she belongs to me."

"Dato," said Sinimory, "the princess is my wife as the king just told you. I ask you to step aside and to no longer seek to disturb this party."

"You lack courage, Sinimory. Come and fight me. The princess will see who is the strongest."

"Wash with this water and drink some. As of today, no spears or bullets will be able to pierce your body," the gorilla leader told Sinimory.

"We can fight," said Sinimory. "I am now king and your last adversary."

Sinimory and Dato fought. The dust they were lifting covered the sky like a cloud. Sweat was pouring down their bodies. The blade of Dato's knife passed over the body of Sinimory without leaving a mark. The tip of Dato's sword touched Sinimory without piercing him. Dato's body was covered in injuries. His spear hit Sinimory but it broke.

"No blade can injure Sinimory." screamed the crowd. "He is a real warrior leader."

Sinimory seized his spear in turn and planted it into Dato's chest who then collapsed. The drums heralded the victory of Sinimory. The griots immediately sang his merits.

"This Sinimory is too strong. He will drive us out of our kingdoms." said the princes who became jealous of him. "He must be poisoned."

"I know an excellent poison." said the king Djougoufala. "Tomorrow at the big party, we will put some in his bottle."

Djanfa, a friend of Sinimory, went to warn him of the intentions of Djougoufala.

The next day during the ceremony, the king Djougoufala placed a bottle at the feet of Sinimory and said to him, "In the name of the kings and princes of the neighboring kingdoms, I offer you the drink of the bride and groom."

"It's nice of you to give me this drink, Djougoufa, but why don't you drink some before I do."

"No, no, Sinimory, this drink is reserved for the groom. I don't have to drink it."

But Sinimory forced Djougoufa to drink. Djougoufa collapsed.

"I'm the strongest," said Sinimory. "Take a good look." And he drank the whole gourd. "Even poison can't do anything against me"

"Sinimory is the greatest of all kings and sorcerers," shouted the people.

Sinimory thus became the greatest king of all time. He had a son whom he named Maméry in memory of his older brother who had been missing since childhood.

One day, Maméry found an old woman sitting in front of the palace. She was asking passerby's for charity to eat and drink. He ran to tell his father. Sinimory sent him to look for her. Sinimory recognized this old woman right away. It was his stepmother.

"Servant," said king Sinimory, "Wash this woman and dress her with some beautiful clothes."

After eating well, the woman came to thank the king.

"I come from a very distant land." she said to Sinimory. "My two sons starved to death and my old husband died of grief."

"Here you are at home." said Sinimory. "You will eat with us tonight."

After the evening meal, the whole palace, including his stepmother, gathered around the king. Maméry sat on his father's lap and said to him, "Baba, take your guitar and sing me 'The Little Dog's Song.'"

"No, not tonight." replied Sinimory.

"Please sing it for me, Baba."

"You must satisfy your son's desire," said the stepmother jokingly to the king.

Sinimory then took his little guitar and began singing:

"Sinimory Oh!

Sinimory, my master,

If your stepmother gives you a plate of rice, do not eat it.

Refuse it, Sinimory, because this dish contains poison.

If your stepmother gives you a plate of sweet potatoes,

Refuse to eat it, Sinimory, because this dish also contains poison.

But if she gives you yam or fonio *dishes,*

Eat them, eat them Sinimory.

And on the day your little Labou will no longer be there to warn you,

The day Labou dies, oh Sinimory,

Go far away from here, Sinimory.

Otherwise the land you clear will eat you."

The stepmother then recognized her son and began to buzz. She buzzed so much that she turned into a big fly. Being overtaken by shame, she vowed to be one of King Sinimory and his family's protectors until the end of time. So, every time servants of the palace served any food, she buzzed and tasted it to make sure it did not contain any poison.

That's why until today, we still have big flies buzzing around trying to be the first to taste the food of good people before we do.

* 9 7 8 1 9 4 7 3 5 0 0 6 9 *